The Man Who Sold His Shadow

retold by Michael Rosen

from the original by
Adelbert von Chamisso

illustrated by Reg Cartwright

LONGMAN

Introduction

Once I found a book in a secondhand bookshop and it was full of poems and stories.

One story was about a man who sold his shadow, written by someone called Chamisso. I thought, "What an amazing idea! Who is this Chamisso anyway?"

I looked him up and discovered that his full name was Adelbert von Chamisso. He had been born in Germany in 1771 and had died in 1838.

The story was written in 1814 and was called "Peter Schlemihls Wunderbare Geschichte" which means "The wonderful story of Peter Schlemihl."

Michael Rosen

The Man Who Sold His Shadow

Peter was a scholar: that meant two things. Firstly he spent all day studying. Secondly he was poor. But today he is lucky. He's got himself invited to see the richest man in town, Mister Thomas.

Mister Thomas was kind enough to look his way for a moment. The rest of the time, he talked with his friends.

"Over there I am going to have built for myself a brand new house – forty rooms, swimming pool, billiard room, cinema... that sort of thing. I'm not ashamed to say it – I'm rich. I couldn't be poor. It would be a misery from morning till night."

"That's true," Peter said to himself.

The moment the thought crossed his mind, at his side was a quiet, thin, lanky, oldish man in a shabby grey coat who looked like the end of a thread that had dropped out of a tailor's needle.

Mister Thomas and his friends walked on round the park, leaving Peter and the strange man alone.

The man spoke first.

"I have only known you for a very short time, but may I say, your shadow is quite the most beautiful shadow I have ever seen in all my life. Excuse me if I am being bold here, but is there any chance that you might sell it to me?"

Peter laughed.

"Isn't your own shadow good enough for you?"

"Then perhaps I could interest you in this?" said the man, and took out a beautiful leather purse.

Peter plunged his hand into it and took out ten gold pieces, and again ten, and again ten, and again ten.

"It's a deal," Peter said. "You have my shadow, and I'll take the purse."

The thin, strange-looking grey man knelt down and gently loosened the shadow from top to toe, rolled it up and put it in his pocket. He then made off towards the trees and soon disappeared amongst them.

• • • • • • • •

Peter was rich but he had no shadow. So what, you might say? Let's see.

He left the park, took the road to the city.

An old woman called after him, "Take care, young man, you've lost your shadow."

"Thanks love," said Peter and threw her a gold coin.

At the city gate, the soldier said, "And where is your shadow, sir?" A woman called out, "Good grief, that feller's got no shadow."

A crowd of children coming out of school gathered round and followed him, laughing and throwing things. Peter broke into a run, the crowds followed. Terrified, he ran through the streets back to his little room.

But there, waiting for him was the woman he loved, Mina. "Where have you been?" she said, "You look awful, darling."

Peter pulled himself together.

"No, no, it's nothing. But listen, Mina. I've got great news. You know I went to see Mister Thomas today. Well, what with one thing and another I'm rich. This means I can go to your parents and ask them if I can marry you."

"Oh you clever thing," said Mina.

Mina's parents were delighted with the rich stranger. Mina's mother whispered in her father's ear, "I'm pretty sure he's a prince, in disguise."

"Of course, you can marry my daughter," said Mina's father later.

Later, as they walked out together, it was noticed that Peter had no shadow.

"Tell me," said the father, "How come you have no shadow?"

"Ah, yes. Of course. One day a rude, clumsy chap trod on it and tore a hole in it. I've sent it off to be mended."

"Very good," said the father. "I tell you what. I'll give you three days to get it back. If after that you have a good, well-fitting shadow, my daughter is yours. If not, she will marry someone else."

Peter was in despair. What could he do? He wandered about wrapped up in his thoughts, more unhappy than he had ever been in all his life. Then, quite unexpectedly, he raised his eyes and saw the old grey man.

Peter grabbed him.

"Give me back my shadow," he said.

"But of course," said the man.
"All you have to do is just sign here
on this piece of paper and your
shadow will return to you."

On the paper were the words:

When I die and my spirit leaves my body, the owner of this paper will be able to have my spirit forever after.

Peter looked more closely at that very same owner of the paper.

"Who are you?"

"Isn't that obvious? A sort of scholar, like you, who tries out a little magic here and there but never gets thanked for it. But no matter, just sign here."

"Never!" shouted Peter. "I'll have nothing more to do with you. I never want to see you again."

And he dug down in his pocket, took out the purse that the old grey man had given him and hurled it into the river.

"Very well," said the man gloomily. "If that's the way you want it..." and without stopping for a moment, he dived into the river after the purse and sank out of sight.

• • • • • • • • •

Peter never saw him again.

So now Peter was poor, he had lost his lover Mina, he had lost his shadow, but at least he had his... at least he had his... Actually he wasn't sure exactly what it was he had, except that he felt more at ease, more peaceful than he had felt for some time.